fenway
AND THE
GREAT ESCAPE

fenway
AND THE
GREAT ESCAPE

VICTORIA J. COE

illustrated by
JOANNE LEW-VRIETHOFF

G. P. PUTNAM'S SONS

G. P. PUTNAM'S SONS
An imprint of Penguin Random House LLC, New York

First published in the United States of America by G. P. Putnam's Sons,
an imprint of Penguin Random House LLC, 2023

Library of Congress Cataloging-in-Publication Data
Names: Coe, Victoria J., author. | Lew-Vriethoff, Joanne, illustrator.
Title: Fenway and the great escape / Victoria J. Coe; illustrated by Joanne Lew-Vriethoff.
Description: New York: G. P. Putnam's Sons, 2023. | Series: Make Way for Fenway |
Summary: Fenway is ecstatic when he is finally allowed off-leash,
until Hattie gets lost and he realizes the leash is mainly to keep her safe.
Identifiers: LCCN 2022050913 (print) | LCCN 2022050914 (ebook) | ISBN 9780593407004
(hardcover) | ISBN 9780593407011 (trade paperback) | ISBN 9780593407028 (epub)
Subjects: CYAC: Jack Russell terrier–Fiction. | Dogs–Fiction. |
Human-animal relationships–Fiction.
Classification: LCC PZ7.1.C635 Fq 2023 (print) | LCC PZ7.1.C635 (ebook) |
DDC [Fic]–dc23
LC record available at https://lccn.loc.gov/2022050913
LC ebook record available at https://lccn.loc.gov/2022050914

Printed in the United States of America

ISBN 9780593407004 (hardcover)

ISBN 9780593407011 (paperback)

1st Printing
LSCC

Design by Cindy De la Cruz | Text set in Bodoni Six ITC Std

For Teddy and Milo.

—V.J.C.

To my forever babies, Max and Mattiece.
Thank you for the amazing adventures and
incredible years. Look forward to more.
I love you.

—J.L.V.

CONTENTS

1

THE HIKE

Want to know what's fun? Hiking in the forest with Hattie and Fetch Man.

And here's some great news—I'm going on a hike today!

I know as soon as I see my short human, Hattie, put her feet into her tie-up boots. Fetch Man does, too.

Then they fill their backpacks with water bottles. And trail mix.

It seems like forever before Hattie grabs my leash and we pile into the car. I'm so ready for our hike!

When we get out of the car, I point my snout in the air. I take in the scents of dirt and pine trees and bug spray. Hooray, we're in the forest!

I love hiking in the forest. There's a trail that goes up hills and down hills. The ground is covered with soft pine needles. And the air is full of sounds, like rustling leaves, singing birds, and some-times other dogs off in the distance.

I can hardly wait to start our hike! I leap and spin.

Hattie sips from her water bottle. Fetch Man bends over to tie his boot. They don't seem to be in any hurry at all. I wish I didn't have to wait for them.

"Hurry up, Hattie! Hurry up, Fetch Man!" I call. I lead them as close to the trail as my short leash will stretch. "Let's start our hike!"

After Hattie fiddles with her backpack and Fetch Man puts on his cap, they begin walking. My tail wags out of control. We're finally heading into the forest.

I guide Hattie and Fetch Man

along, my tail high and proud. My ears are perked. It's my job to protect Hattie from wild animals like squirrels. And lucky for her, I'm a professional.

Right now, the forest is peaceful. Branches sway in the breeze. A bird tweets a happy song. But I know that could change at any moment. A sneaky squirrel might come scampering toward my Hattie. I have to be ready to save her.

Since she's just on the other end of the leash, I'm here to protect her. A squirrel would have to be nuts to mess with a tough dog like me.

Even so, it's a good idea to send

out a warning. "Leave my short human alone, Squirrels!" I call out.

As we walk farther along the trail, I don't hear any squirrels chippering or chattering or squawking. Did my barking scare them off? Or are they quietly getting ready to strike?

We climb up a hill. We clomp down the other side. Hiking is fun, but there's no time to relax. I have a job to do!

Around a turn, we come to a clearing where I hear noises. My tail goes wild. Those noises belong to dogs. Lots of dogs!

I romp into the clearing. Hattie's

right on my tail. "Fenway!" she cries.

When we get deeper into the clearing, my tail goes even wilder. Up ahead, I see a group of dogs playing chase without me.

2

FREEDOM

Wait for me, everybody!" I call out to the other dogs. "I'll be right over!"

The other dogs are having so much fun, they don't even notice me. I try to race to them, but thanks to my leash, I don't get very far.

"You can't catch me!" a Golden

Doodle taunts the others. He leaps over a rock. Wowee, he's speedy.

"That's what you think!" cries a Pug. She makes a sharp turn and heads the Doodle off.

He pivots and goes the other way. A brown dog with short hair speeds after him. "I'm going to get you first!"

I let out a whimper. Those other dogs are having so much fun without me. I can't just stand here and watch.

I turn around. "I've got a great idea, Hattie," I bark. "Let's go over there to the other dogs."

Hattie responds by trying to steer me back to the trail, where Fetch Man is waiting. "This way, Fenway," she mutters.

I gaze up at Hattie with my saddest face. "Come on," I whine. "Don't you want me to have fun?"

But Hattie keeps walking.

She must not get how important this is. What's wrong with her?

I try not to watch those dogs and their game. I try not to listen. But I can't help seeing the Pug nearly catch the Doodle, who darts away at the last second. "Ha! I'll get you next time!" the Pug calls.

And that's when I notice something big. The other dogs are running around without leashes!

I gaze up at mine. Suddenly, I realize that Hattie is not the problem. The leash is! I need to get rid of it.

If I didn't have this leash, I could run off and join those other dogs. Hattie and Fetch Man could keep on hiking, and I could catch up with them whenever I want. It's the Best Idea Ever!

I sneer at the leash. I open my jaws. I clamp my teeth down and give it a big *CHOMP!*

"Fenway," Hattie scolds. She sounds like Food Lady when she uses her "you're in trouble" voice.

I let the leash go, my tail drooping. What did I do?

"Come," she says. She continues marching to the trail and Fetch Man.

I have to try harder. I growl at the leash. I bite into it. I pull with all my might.

Hattie points a finger at me. "No tug-of-war," she snaps.

If she thinks I'm playing the tug-of-war game, then she must remember that I always win. I dig in my hind legs. I pull and pull and pull.

A few moments later, I see Fetch Man talking to Hattie. I can't tell what he's saying, but Hattie tilts her head and nods. She gives me a warning glance, and I notice a sparkle in her eye.

My tail springs up. I
know that look. She's about
to give in! I knew she would!

"Fenway, sit," she commands.

After another peek over at
the romping dogs, I drop to the
ground. Hattie's reaching for my
collar. And the leash.

I wait for the
sound—*click*—and
then I take off.

3

TREATS!

Whoopee! I'm free!

I race deeper into the clearing. I'm speeding toward those other dogs. I'm so excited! But as I leap over a big stick, a strong odor stops me in my tracks. *Sniff . . . sniff . . .* squirrels!

Nose to the ground, I follow the scent to a big tree. Its roots are

covered with moss.
And the horrible
stench of rodent. I
must investigate!

I'm so busy
sniffing, I almost
don't hear Hattie
calling.

"Fenway, oh, Fenway," she sings in her sweet voice. When I whip around, I see her holding out her hand like she wants me to come get something yummy.

Yippee! That can only be one thing! My tail shoots up, and I romp over. "I'm so hungry!" I bark. "Give me that treat!"

As soon as I get to Hattie, I sink onto my bum. I smack my chops. I gaze up at her in that cute way she likes.

Hattie opens her hand and—
PLUNK—the treats drop into my
mouth.

CHOMP! *Mmmmm*. Yahoo, was
that ever tasty!

Hattie pats my head. "Good job," she says. Fetch Man smiles.

Aw, shucks. They're probably glad I'm still on guard against squirrels. "Don't worry, Hattie," I bark. "Even though I can go wherever I want, I'm always on alert."

As she's scratching my back, the brown dog's yips reach my ears. "I'm gonna get you!" he calls to the others.

I spin around, my tail going nuts. I almost forgot that I haven't joined the fun. "Hold on, everybody!" I cry, rushing toward them. "I'm coming!"

Up ahead, the Golden Doodle and the Pug are romping in circles. The brown dog darts back and forth, like he can't decide which one to chase.

I can't wait to play the game. My legs are flying! I'm almost there!

But a step or two later, that strong odor hits my nose again. *Sniff . . . sniff . . .* more squirrels!

I track that smell to another tree. Its trunk reeks of rodent. Those squirrels are nearby. And they're probably ready to attack. I have to protect my short human.

I'm following their scent partway back into the clearing when

I hear Hattie
calling again.

"Fenway, oh, Fenway,"
she sings. Her voice is
even sweeter this time.

Her timing is terrible. But
I can't say no to a tasty snack!

I spy Hattie and Fetch
Man at the other end of the
clearing. I gallop over, my
tail swishing. "I'm so ready
for that treat!" I bark.

When I get to them, I plop down in the pine needles. That morsel is in my mouth a second later. Yum!

The same thing happens again and again. Hattie must be awfully happy I'm keeping her safe, because she gives me treat after treat. Each time I come back for the snack, she pats my head and tells me what a good job I'm doing. How awesome is that?

By the time we're out of the clearing and back on the trail, I've eaten more treats than I can count. And the other dogs are nowhere in sight.

4

THE LADIES

On the ride home, I have more energy than ever. I climb all over Hattie in the back seat. Wowee, it's so good to be free!

"Can you believe how many squirrels I saved you from?" I bark at Hattie. As we spill out of the car and barrel into the house, I'm leaping on her legs nonstop.

"Aw, Fenway," Hattie says with a giggle. She rubs my neck. She's obviously very proud of me.

Fetch Man is not giggling. He's shaking his head. "Outside," he says to us.

Next thing I know, Hattie's sliding open the back door. I race out into the Dog Park. That's the grassy space behind our house that's surrounded by a fence. I speed down the steps.

After making sure the Dog Park is free of squirrels—and watering the bushes—I hear jingling dog tags. Hooray! Hooray! That means my friends Goldie and Patches are out in their Dog Park next door.

"'Sup, ladies?" I call, trotting over to the side fence.

"Is that you, Fenway?" Patches says in her lovely voice. I spy Goldie lumbering up behind her.

"It sure is." I thrust out my chest. "And I have some big news!"

"Let me guess," Goldie grumbles. "You got another bone? Or a Frisbee?"

"Much bigger than that," I tell them.

"How exciting, Fenway," Patches says, bouncing. "What's the news?"

I stand a bit taller. "I don't need a leash anymore!"

Goldie's mouth falls open. "Really?" she cries.

Patches cocks her head. "Why do you think that?"

I strut back and forth, my tail high and wagging. "I don't think—I *know*," I brag. "Me and Hattie were hiking in the forest, and I convinced her to take my leash off."

The ladies exchange a questioning look. Goldie is the first to turn back to me. "You ran around without a leash?"

"Leashes are important, you know," Patches says gently. "They help keep dogs safe."

"Especially certain dogs," Goldie adds.

"Maybe leashes are important for some dogs," I say. "But not for me. I was safe the whole time, and nothing bad happened."

"Good for you, Fenway," Patches says. Her eyes look like she's happy for me, but her voice doesn't sound so sure. "Did you have fun running off-leash?"

I drop down for a scratch. "I sure did! But it could've been even better if sneaky squirrels hadn't been everywhere."

Patches stares. "Well, it was a forest."

"Wait a minute—was this like the time when your leash ripped in half?" Goldie asks with a snort. "Or are you saying your short human was actually okay with you off the leash?"

"I'm telling you, I convinced Hattie to unclip it. And she was better than okay. She gave me loads of treats!" I gaze into Goldie's eyes. She still looks like she doesn't believe me. "Ladies, my days of being stuck on that leash are over. From now on, I'm going wherever I want."

5

THE DREAM

That night, me and Hattie are curled up in her bed. She smells like mint and vanilla, like always. But unlike always, I don't feel sleepy.

Whoopee, it was so great being off that leash! Even now, lying in Hattie's cozy blankets, my legs still feel like they're running. My fur still feels rumpled from the breeze.

My tail is still thumping with that wonderful feeling of freedom.

I start to imagine all the places I can go without being stuck on the leash—the Treat Place, the Big Park, the forest . . . I could even chase the Big Brown Truck away.

I must lie awake half the night thinking of all the awesome things I can do without that no-good leash. But eventually, my eyes blink shut . . .

I'm back in the forest with my family—Food Lady, Fetch Man, and Hattie. They're hiking along the trail while I romp ahead. Far ahead. I feel so free, like the entire forest is mine.

My humans stay on the trail, but who

says that I have to stay with them? Nobody, that's who! I go where I want. I chase squirrels. I play with other dogs. No leash is holding me back.

I run for a long, long time. There's no trail, and who cares? I'm having so much fun, I could run forever and ever.

I can hear leaves rustling, birds singing, and chipmunks chipping.

Also, squirrels—way too many squirrels.

CHIPPER-CHATTER-SQUAWK!

I turn around and there they are. Hundreds of squirrels! Maybe more! They're scampering toward a trail and some humans. It's Food Lady, Fetch Man, and Hattie!

"Don't go near my family, Squirrels!" I whine. "Or else . . ."

But the squirrels keep heading to the trail!

EEE-YAH! They're going to get my humans!

6

THE WALK

Just then, I wake up. Morning light shines through Hattie's window. She's sliding her feet into her shoes. Whew! Thank goodness I kept her safe.

I follow Hattie into the Eating Place. She sits at the table and crunches on toast that smells like butter. I perch at her feet, catching the bits of crust she drops into my mouth whenever Food Lady looks away.

I'm swallowing a delicious buttery bite when—*DING-DONG!*

The doorbell!

I blast into the hall and head for the door. "Watch out, Intruders!" I bark. "A Jack Russell Terrier is on patrol!"

But when Hattie opens the door, my ears flap down and my tail swings happily.

It's not intruders. It's our friend Angel! Goldie and Patches stand beside her on their matching leashes.

"Ready?" Angel asks.

"I'm so ready! I'm so ready!" I bark. I leap and spin. I'm going for a walk with Hattie and my best friends! This is the Best Day Ever!

I'm ready to burst through the door when I hear a familiar sound—*click*.

The leash?!

I look up at her. "We're not using that anymore," I bark. "Remember?"

Hattie doesn't answer. Instead, we head outside as if everything is

fine. She starts chatting with Angel
like she didn't even hear me.

We trot toward the street behind
our short humans.

"Good morning, Fenway," says
Patches.

Goldie gives me a nod. "What's up with the leash? Thought you were done with that."

"I am," I tell her. "I think Hattie needs some reminding."

We stop at a tree, and the ladies get busy sniffing. I turn to Hattie. "Forgetting something?" I bark.

Hattie reaches down and pats my head, but she's not listening to me. She just keeps chatting with Angel.

Clearly, I need to change my strategy. I give the leash a *CHOMP!* and begin tugging.

That gets her attention. "Fenway!" she cries in a surprised voice. She wags her finger at me. "No leash!"

Finally, she understands! I let the leash drop.

But Hattie doesn't unclip it. She just turns to Angel and gets back to chatting.

Patches gazes up from sniffing. "Leashes aren't so bad, Fenway," she says. "We still get to stop and smell all the neighborhood smells."

"What's the big deal?" Goldie says. "We're out for a walk together. You don't want to run off on us, do you?"

I look away. The ladies don't get it. It's not that I *want* to be someplace else. It's the idea that if it weren't for this no-good leash, I *could be*.

I chomp the leash again. This time, I tug harder. I give it all I've got.

Hattie whips around. "Fenway!" she snaps. Her face is angry. "Stop it!"

My ears droop and my teeth unclench. Why is Hattie upset? I'm the one who's trapped on the leash. For now, anyway.

7

THE FOREST

A few days later, I see Hattie and Fetch Man strap on their backpacks. They're wearing their tie-up boots. Yippee! We're headed to the forest for another hike!

Yes! It's my chance to show Hattie once and for all that I don't need that leash.

"Hooray! Hooray!" I bark. "I love hiking!" I sprint to the car before Hattie can grab the leash.

But once we're together in the back seat—*click*—I hear that awful sound. I tell myself that this is how it started before. Hattie needs a reminder, that's all.

When the car stops and we scramble out, I sniff the air. The smells of dirt and pine trees and bug spray tell me what I already know—we're back in the forest.

Hattie holds on to the leash while she and Fetch Man buckle their backpacks. I shouldn't have to stay here and wait for them. I should be sprinting up and down the hills, tearing through the soft pine needles, and chasing wild animals. I'm so ready!

"Hurry up!" I bark at Hattie, jumping on her legs. "Take off the leash!"

"Fenway," she grumbles. "Down."

The good news is that we're strolling up to the trail at last. The bad news is that the end of the leash is tight in her hand.

I need to keep trying. A few steps later, I plop onto my bum. I chomp the leash. When Hattie turns around, I look up at her with a sad face. I give the leash a tug or two in case she doesn't get it.

Hattie gazes over at Fetch Man. Her shoulders scrunch up around her ears.

My tail thumps. That's the look! She's giving in!

Hattie glances down at me.

"Fenway, wait," she says.

I want to leap up so bad! But Hattie told me to wait on my bum.

Hattie leans over and reaches for my collar. A moment later—*click*. I'm free! Yippee!

I take off, my ears perked for sounds. My nose is primed for scents. I dash. I dart. I zig and zag down the trail. I'm leaping into the brush when I hear Hattie's sweet voice.

"Fenway, oh, Fenway!"

I spin around. She's holding her hand out. I know what that means!

I bolt back to Hattie and drop to my bum. **CHOMP!** *Mmmmm.*

As soon as I've swallowed the yummy treat, I take off again. I've got the whole forest to explore! Yahoo!

I rush through sticks. I hop over rocks. I wiggle under a fallen tree trunk. Wowee!

I've started charging toward the clearing up ahead when I spy the flick of a bushy tail.

It can only be one thing—a squirrel!

I'm after him in a flash. No squirrel can outrun me!

In the distance I hear Hattie's sweet voice. "Fenway, oh, Fenway!"

She probably wants to give me another treat. But I can eat treats anytime. Right now I have a sneaky squirrel to chase.

8

PLAYTIME

The bushy tail keeps flicking in the same spot. Doesn't that squirrel realize I'm onto him?

I tear into the clearing, my teeth bared. "Get out of here, Rodent!" I bark. "I know you're up to no good!"

I'm almost close enough to pounce when he looks up. Then

he suddenly turns
and scampers toward
the nearest pine tree.

I pick up my speed. "I'm
warning you for
the last time!"
I bark.

He hops over
a root and scurries
up the trunk in the
nick of time. His
teasing floats
down from the
branches.

CHIPPER-CHATTER-SQUAWK!

I leap onto my hind legs, my front paws gripping the bark. "Now stay there!"

Whew.

I'm about to get back to exploring when I hear the jingle of dog tags somewhere behind me. I whip around and head back into the clearing.

"I dare you to chase me!" one doggy voice calls.

"Over here!" cries another.

As I sprint deeper into the clearing, I spy two dogs—a Pitbull and a Yellow Lab—romping on their own. And they look like they're having a blast!

"Great news, everybody!" I shout, galloping over. "I'm ready to join in the fun!"

The Pitbull pivots. The Lab races after her. The chase is on!

I dash after the Lab. He's right on the Pitbull's tail. Whoopee! This game of chase is awesome!

But right when the Yellow Lab is about to catch her, the Pitbull rolls onto her back. The Lab flops down beside her. "I need a rest," the Pitbull says, panting.

The Yellow Lab's tongue hangs out of his mouth. "Me too," he says.

When I reach them, we exchange bum sniffs. They tell me their names are Teddy and Milo. "It's so awesome to be done with silly leashes," I say, dashing from one dog to the other. "Right?"

They share a puzzled look. Milo gazes up at me first. "Done?"

Teddy wrinkles her snout. "Silly?"

I run in circles around them. "I don't miss the leash at all," I say. "I'm on my own. I go where I want. You two know what I mean?"

"A little bit," Milo mutters. He reminds me of Goldie.

"I run without a leash sometimes," says Teddy. "But not always." She sounds like Patches.

I cock my head in surprise. "We've got total freedom!" I say.

"What's not to love?"

But before they can answer, voices sound across the clearing. Human voices.

"MILO!" one yells.

"TEDDY!" shouts the other.

The dogs pop up like the ground's on fire. They take off to the other end of the clearing.

"Gotta go!" Milo cries.

"See ya!" Teddy hollers.

"Bye," I call after them. And just like that, I'm alone.

Well, that wasn't as fun as I thought it would be. But this forest is huge. There must be other amazing things to do.

I charge to the far side of the clearing, romping and sniffing and checking things out. At some point, I stop and listen for Hattie. But I can't hear her at all.

9

LOST?

I race past trees, looking in every direction. I can't smell Hattie. And I don't see any sign of her. But she must be nearby. I can't have gone that far.

Is this even the right direction? Maybe Hattie's waiting for me back in the clearing.

That must be it!

I spin around and run the other way. I pass trees and logs. And more trees and logs. The clearing is supposed to be up ahead. So where is it?

I turn to one side, then the other. All I see are trees. I can't tell which way is out.

A tingle shoots up and down my back. Am I lost?

"Hattie!" I call. "Hattie?" I perk my ears and listen.

But she doesn't answer. Nobody answers.

"Hattie! Hattie?" I call again. This time, I listen even harder.

She still doesn't answer. Where is she?

I romp in different directions. I'm going in circles. My fur prickles as a terrifying thought pops into my head.

What if Hattie's the one who's lost? What if she's afraid of all the squirrels? What if she's in trouble?

She needs her loyal dog. I have to find her!

I'm rounding another circle when I hear the rustle of leaves and cracks of twigs.

It must be Hattie!

I rush toward the sounds. "I'm coming, Hattie!" I race through the brush and down a slope.

I splash through a trickling

stream. I squish in a patch of mud. Nothing will stop me. I have to find Hattie!

But nobody's around. "Hattie?" I cry more sharply. "Hattie?"

I lumber up a little hill. At the top, I pick up speed. I'm loping toward a giant rock when my ears prick.

I hear a voice on the other side. Maybe it's Hattie!

My tail swings in triumph. "Don't worry, Hattie, you're not lost anymore," I bark. "I found you!"

But as I reach the other side of the giant rock, all I see are a tall human and two short humans. Strangers.

I turn one way, then the other. Where is Hattie?

One of the short humans reaches her hand toward me. "Hey, doggy."

My tail sags and I back away. "Never mind," I whimper.

I have to get out of here. I turn and sprint away from the humans who are not Hattie. Up ahead, I see sunlight shining through a gap in the trees. Is that the clearing? Or maybe the trail?

I race toward it. But as I get closer, there is no clearing. There is no trail. Just trees, trees, and more trees.

I pull to a stop, panting. High overhead, there's a shuffling sound. It could be Hattie. She could've climbed the tree.

I gaze up into the branches. "Is that you, Hattie?" I yelp. "Are you up there?"

But instead of Hattie's sweet voice, I hear **CHIPPER-CHATTER-SQUAWK!**

Sneaky squirrels!

I take a few steps backward. I'm shivering all over. What if it gets dark? What if it rains and there are loud **BOOM-KABOOMS**? Hattie would be so scared without me.

I sink down in a heap. Hattie's

lost and afraid of squirrels. She needs me to protect her. This is the Worst Day Ever.

But as I lie in the pine needles, I hear a faraway voice call, "Fenway?!" The voice sounds afraid. And it sounds like Hattie.

10

CLICK

I tilt my head. I listen with all my might.

"Fenway?! Fenway?!"

My tail shoots up. It IS Hattie!

I sprint toward her voice. I race past trees, trees, and more trees. I rush through brush and twigs and pine needles.

Up ahead, I see an opening.

"Fenway?! Fenway?!" Her voice is getting louder. Closer.

"Don't be scared, Hattie! I'm coming!" I bark. I blast through the opening in the trees. And as I reach the trail, my tail begins swinging in circles. Someone's coming around the bend. I spy a short human with bushy hair. A leash is dangling from her hand. It's Hattie!

When Hattie sees me, her eyes get bigger. She breaks into a run. "Fenway!" she cries.

"It's okay, Hattie," I bark, rushing to her. "I'm here, and you don't need to be afraid of squirrels anymore."

Hattie holds out her arms. Her grin is as wide as her whole face. "Fenway!" She scoops me up and rocks me back and forth. She showers me with kisses.

I snuggle against her chest. And when I hear that familiar sound—*click*—I finally start to relax.

The next day, me and Hattie are going for a walk. I wait at the door for the *click*, and then we burst outside.

At the end of the driveway, we meet up with Angel and the ladies. My snout is high, my chest is out, and my tail is tall and proud.

Patches nuzzles my neck as we head up the street. "You seem awfully perky today, Fenway," she says in her lovely voice.

Goldie gives me a nod. "What's up?" she asks. "I thought you were done with that leash."

I gaze up at my short human. She's chattering away with Angel, happy as always. I turn back to my friends. "You'll never guess what I learned," I say.

Goldie and Patches look at each other, then at me. "Probably not," Goldie mumbles.

"Tell us, Fenway," Patches says.

I slow my steps so I'm in line with Hattie. "It turns out the leash isn't for ME," I tell the ladies. "It's for HATTIE. So she won't get lost. Or scared."

As we keep on walking, Goldie and Patches are quiet, like they're thinking it over.

We stop at our favorite tree, and we dogs go in for a sniff. I hear a sneaky squirrel start to clatter down the trunk.

I leap up with a growl. "Keep your distance," I bark. "Nobody gets near Hattie when I'm around."

He freezes. Then he turns and scurries back into the branches.

I glance at the leash. Hattie's right at the other end. I give a happy sigh. This leash is pretty good after all.

ABOUT THE AUTHOR

VICTORIA J. COE's books for middle grade readers include the Global Read Aloud, Amazon Teachers' Pick, and One School, One Book favorite *Fenway and Hattie* as well as three Fenway and Hattie sequels. **Make Way for Fenway!** is her first chapter book series. Connect with her online at victoriajcoe.com and on Twitter and Instagram @victoriajcoe.

ABOUT THE ILLUSTRATOR

JOANNE LEW-VRIETHOFF's passion and love for storytelling is shown through her whimsical and heartfelt illustrations in picture and chapter books. Joanne also loves dis-

covering the world with her family by traveling and collecting memories along the way, giving her more inspiration for her illustrations. Her favorite downtime activities are reading YA books recommended by her daughter, looking at TikTok videos of dogs and cats, and watching the Discovery Channel. Currently, Joanne divides her time between Amsterdam and Asia. Connect with her on Instagram @joannelewvriethoff.

LOOK FOR ALL OF THE

MAKE WAY FOR FENWAY!

CHAPTER BOOKS!